A Melody of Love

A Melody of Love

Lori Ellett Street

Copyright © 2001 by Lori Ellett Street
All rights reserved. No part of this book may be reproduced, stored in a retrieval system, or transmitted by any means, electronic, mechanical, photocopying, recording, or otherwise, without written permission from the author.

ISBN: 0-75961-012-6

This book is printed on acid free paper.

1stBooks - rev. 2/17/01

This book is dedicated to my mother and father (Marlin and Kathy Ellett) for without their encouragement not a single word would have been written.

And in memory of my grandmother,
Ada McFarland Ellett

A Melody of love

The rooster crowed with much enthusiasm, more than anyone could say for Melody Jones.

"Why, oh why, do you insist on performing that horrid sound every morning?" Melody groaned as if the rooster would feel threatened. She covered her head with the pillow and mumbled to herself. I should catch that old rooster and put him in a pot for dinner. But, Melody would never harm the old red top rooster. She knew her mother dearly loved it.

The sun was just coming in through the sheers in her bedroom window. Already the light beaming in, brightened every corner of her room. "No, no, sun go away!" she groaned again.

"Melody!" her mother yelled from downstairs. "Breakfast is ready!" Her mother didn't like it when anyone was late at mealtimes.

Melody took the pillow off her head and sat up straight on her bed. Her beautiful auburn hair was in an array of a mess.

"What's the point in getting up," she said to herself? "There is nothing to do. What could be more boring than spending life on this dreadful farm in Indiana?

"Melody," her mother yelled again. In the kitchen her mother was helping with Melody's two younger brothers. Her dad had already begun his day an hour or so ago, and was in the fields by now. "I'll never figure that girl out," her mother mumbled to Ben age five and Eli age seven. Melody was ten years older than her oldest brother Eli. Her mother had two miscarriages between them. "Any girl, who wants to sleep in on a beautiful day like this, is unlike anything I've ever seen. If it wasn't for Murphy, I don't think she would ever leave her room," mumbled her mother more.

"I bet Melody is going to be an old maid," laughed Eli.

"None of that, scolded their mother, your sister is a beautiful young lady. She'll be fine. But I do wish she could find a hobby or something to keep her content."

"I heard that Eli!" said Melody as she made her way slowly into the kitchen. "So what if I chose not to marry. A lot of women stay single and are very happy. Besides I'll never find anyone who suits me in this dull place," said Melody.

"Melody, there are a lot of nice boys around. I'm sure this fall at school you'll find some that interest you. You know boys change a lot when they get your age. You just need to keep an open mind," assured her mother.

Melody just sat there, shook her head, and rolled her golden brown eyes as she took a bite of bacon. She thought to herself, what hope did she have in finding a beau. It was her last year of school. Some boys in their area had already left for the military. Slim pickings she thought. Maybe she was going to be an old maid. But, that might not be so bad. I could travel. And the only one I would have to please would be myself. I could go any where I desired, and no one would care.

"Mother, may we be excused?" said Eli and Ben almost the same time. They always found something to do on the farm. To them it seemed there aren't enough hours in the day.

"Yes, she said, Just make sure you do your chores and be in for supper."

"Yes, mother, we'll be in at six o'clock for supper," Eli replied. All the children and their father knew that mother insisted everyone be in promptly at six o'clock for the evening meal together. They often teased her about it. But, actually everyone enjoyed the family together.

Melody thought about school. She would enjoy the chance to read some different books, and chatting with Ada. Ada McFarland was her best friend. She only got to talk to her on sundays in the summer, and that was only a few minutes just before or after church. But, school also meant seeing more of Ada's pesky brother John. He was always bothering her. Putting frogs in her seat, pulling her hair, anything, he could do to annoy her. How could anyone be such a pain, she thought to herself? Not only that, his name was as dull as they come. Practically every family in Indiana had a John in it. She herself had a cousin and an uncle named John. If she ever had a son, she would insist his name be something original. Like Chester or something. Then her thoughts turned back to Ada. Now there was a prize. She was beautiful. Every boy's dream. She had shiny black hair with perfect long curls in the back, and big green eyes. Poor Ada, Melody thought, she will never be able to find a suitor as handsome as she deserved, not here anyway. But, for some reason Ada didn't seem to be bothered by that. She was always happy, almost flirtatiously. Nearly as if she liked the boys hanging around her. Oh, well she'll have to deal with that herself. But as for me, I don't see any opportunity for me here.

"Melody!" said her mother. Melody's heart nearly jumped out of her. She was so caught up in thinking that she had forgotten about eating. "Stop daydreaming and finish your breakfast. Go outside and enjoy this beautiful day that the Lord has made. It's not good for you to spend all of your time inside."

"Yes, mother," she said. But how could she find anything interesting to do on this lonely farm, she asked herself. She was not about to join her brothers on their silly adventures.

Just then her mother said, "Be in by six o'clock and don't forget to gather the eggs.

Oh yes, thought Melody, that will be the highlight of my day. Sliding my hand under an ole fat hen to rob form it's nest. Was this all that life had to offer in Indiana? Was she to become some sort of professional egg gather? She laughed to herself.

Melody tired to busy herself outside. She strolled around the farm looking at all the animals. Poor cows, they never go beyond the fences. All their lives' hold is whatever happens on this farm. She looked around to see if any cats had new kittens. But, mostly her day was filled with talking to Murphy. Murphy was the farm's sad eyed looking blood hound. He had been Melody's birthday gift two years ago.

"Oh Murphy, you look as miserable as I feel. Don't you wish we had the chance to go somewhere different, somewhere with more opportunity?" she said as she patted him on the head.

"Maybe like Chicago. But, I suppose you would feel it was too noisy. Although I think, I might enjoy it. Oh, well so much for now, I really don't think I could possibly leave. What with no source of income and a year of school left. I'll just think of tomorrow, when I get to see Ada at church. Maybe she'll have something interesting to talk about. I sure hope John doesn't go. Maybe he'll get the measles or something." She looked down at the dog, who tilted its head to the side as if he knew what Melody had said. "I know Murphy, God doesn't want us to wish bad things on people. I take it back. Oh, Murphy, I wish everyone could be as sweet as you."

◡

Sunday had come. At least today Melody didn't mind getting out of bed. It was fun to see all the people. She wondered, who would have new dresses on? What would the sermon be? And most of all what would Ada have to say? Ada always seemed to have some interesting news of some sort. Maybe that's why Melody liked her so well. She often wandered just how Ada got her news so fast. She seemed to know things as soon as they happened. It must be because they have a telephone and we don't pondered Melody. Not many homes had telephones. Oh, wouldn't that be fun, listening in on the party lines, she thought. But for now she would have to rely on Ada's reports at church. Her only wish is that Murphy could join them. It would be fun to see the heads turn, she thought. He would really light up the place.

Melody and her family arrived at church. Her eyes scattered around for signs of Ada.

"Boo!" the sound came from behind her. She turned around to see Ada smiling from ear to ear.

"Ada, you scared me," Melody said jokingly. "Why are you so full of sunshine today, Ada? A new beau maybe?"

"No, better than that," Ada said "It's John!"

"Oh, my, he doesn't have the measles, does he?" Melody asked fearfully. Had her secret wish come true?

"Lands no, silly," laughed Ada. "He went to my uncle's in Peoria Illinois. My uncle injured his arm and needs John to help out. Can you imagine, the whole summer without my pesky brother around? It feels too good to be true."

Well at least someone was happy about summer, Melody thought. She dazed all the way home about John. What was it like in Peoria? Was it lonely like the farm she lived on? Would he have neighbors close by? As Melody thought she came up with the idea she was actually jealous John was going to Peoria. Oh, why didn't life bring her opportunities like that.

Her summer days crept by. She spent endless hours talking over life with Murphy. Melody also had to so her share in the family's huge garden. She hated the mindful work of pulling weeds. Often she feared she would mistake a plant for a weed. But, her mother was always there working right along with her. And besides they had to keep a large garden for the necessary winter food supply.

"Melody, her mother said, you spend so much time with Murphy. Do you think you would care to find a hobby? I could teach you to cross stitch or maybe we could find a paint set for you. I'm sure you Aunt Rose could send you one from Bloomington. It really might do you some good to find more things that interest you."

"I'm really not interested in either mother. If you really want to know, I am interested in moving to a city. Somewhere without cows, pigs, annoying roosters and acres and acres of corn," replied Melody.

"What would you do when you got to the city?" her mother questioned. "I really hadn't thought of that," Melody softly said. As she pulled weeds, she thought. No, she hadn't any idea of what she would do in the city, she just figured that it would have to be more interesting than the farm. Even John McFarland, went to another state. But, all the talk of what John wrote in his letters to home, seemed to Melody that Peoria sounded much like

Indiana. She looked over at Murphy, who was walking the rows beside her.

"You don't suppose, do you Murphy that even Peoria is as dull as this farm? Oh dear, what if everywhere is like Indiana, and I'm the dull one?" Melody wandered to herself. It might be that all places are much like the farm. Other people she knew seemed content. But why didn't she. She longed for adventure. Any kind of adventure that would be different from farm life.

The whole week Melody worked in the garden. Murphy was always beside her. Her mother often worried that the dog would trample the plants. But, he seemed to understand that he was only to lie in between the plant rows. Melody was glad for his company.

Sunday at church Ada had some news. She said that John wrote he would be home by the first day of school. Ada seemed as if she was excited John were coming home. The first day of school was just two weeks away.

Her mother was busy making dresses for Melody and shirts and pants for Eli. Ben wasn't quite old enough for school yet. Melody wandered if Ben would find the farm as lonely as she did. She and Eli would no longer be home during the day, and Ben was so used to having Eli around.

"Mother, do you think Ben will think the farm is boring after Eli and I start school?" questioned Melody.

"Dear, not all people feel farm life is dull. Some of us find it very rewarding," her mother explained.

Melody thought, how could doing the same chores day in and day out, be rewarding? Never going beyond the little community close to your home for weeks at a time.

"Oh, well to each his own, she mumbled to herself. But, I'll never live on a farm when I get of age.

The next week was busy. It was filled with getting the clothes ready. And most of all instructing Eli on how to act properly in school. She did hope that her brother would not act as some of the mischievous boys at school did.

◡

The school bell rang, just as Eli and Melody made their way up the stairs. It never occurred to her that she should have left earlier with Eli than when she walked by herself. Eli seemed to stop and look at everything. How embarrassing she thought, to be tardy on the first day? She was relieved to see a few other children running up the steps past her. They ran in front of her and got all the seats except one. That was the one in front of John McFarland. Oh, no how much worse can it get? Almost tardy and now seating in front of John. He'll probably bother me so much I'll never get my lessons. I should just walk out and never return. What's the point in staying if I never learn? She thought. I was looking so forward to school, and now this. Just then Melody noticed the teacher had loudly cleared her throat and everyone was staring at her. How long had she been daydreaming, she thought?

"Miss, please stand and say your name as the others have done," the teacher said sternly.

"Oh yes, of course," said Melody. She rose and stated her name Melody Jones, than quickly sat down. She thought to herself, things have just got worse. I have got to stop daydreaming.

"John McFarland," he said. Melody turned and looked up at him. Was it really John. He must have grown six inches and his voice sounded different. Why hadn't she noticed his brown eyes before, she thought? Mother said boys changed when they got my age. Yet she never expected this. She must have been staring at him strangely, because when he returned to his seat, he winked at her.

Of all the nerve, Melody thought, winking at me. As if he thought I'd get some thrill of it. Well did she get a thrill? She asked herself. Of course not, she told herself. He's a pest and a dull farmer at that. I can't believe he winked, what did it mean? All day long she could not even bring herself to look at him, for fear that he would wink at her once more.

As Melody walked home, she thought to herself. John didn't bother me once today, only the wink. Which I guess wasn't too bad. No frogs, no hair pulls, and at lunch I noticed he was sitting over by the tree studying. We'll I'm sure he was just thinking of some tricks. I'll bet tomorrow he'll be full of pranks. Yelp, I bet he was planning a big prank and needed to study it though.

As the school days continued John never attempted to bother her. In fact he always treated her very nicely. If they both got to the door the same time, he would let her go first. Once he offered to carry her books home. But, she was so shy, that her excuse was, she must get home quickly and do her chores. Although it would have been tempting. She never had her books carried for her before. She thought about asking Ada what was up with John. But, she knew Ada would ask why she cared so much. She would probably accuse her of liking John. No, I'll not ask Ada, she told herself. Maybe I'll just talk it over with Murphy.

Sunday came and Ada meet Melody at the door.

"Ask your Ma and Pa if you can come over to our house for dinner. My uncle is here from Peoria. We are having a special dinner for him," Ada said. Melody was delighted she was invited. Since Ada had been dating Ray Harris, the two hardly had a chance to talk. She was sure her parents would not mind. She often had dinner at the McFarlands just as Ada had at hers.

Melody's mother and father agreed and soon she found herself at the McFarland farm. It wasn't much different than that of her family's. They had the same types of animals and grew the same crops.

"Melody lets go in the hayloft. I know where a cat is hiding her kittens," Ada said excitedly. Ever since the girls had been little, they often search for kittens. They enjoyed dressing them in doll clothes when they were younger. Now that they were grown up, they just liked to pet the kittens and talk. So off they went. While they were in the loft, John, his father, and uncle came into the barn.

Ada whispered to Melody, "Don't make a sound, I don't want them to know we are here."

"But that's eavesdropping!" whispered Melody.

"I know, Ada said, but my uncle didn't come all the way from Peoria just for dinner. I want to find out what's up."

Ada's uncle told John and his father that he was moving into the town part of Peoria to run the hardware store. He just couldn't care for the farm after his arm injury, the uncle was saying. Since he had no children he thought John would like to take it off his hands. From the way John grinned, Melody was sure he would accept.

Ada and Melody sunk down in the hay, as the men left to continue the conversation outside.

"Just imagine, said Ada, our John will be living in Peoria and have his very own farm."

"I wish I was going to Peoria, Melody replied, but not as a farmer." John was so lucky, thought

Melody. Having the chance to leave Indiana must be exciting.

When Melody returned home, she had a long talk with Murphy. “I just can’t image going all the way to Illinois, just to work a farm. If I had that chance, I’d sell the farm and head toward a more exciting place. That’s exactly what I’d do. Of course I would take you,” she said while hugging Murphy.

The next day after school John caught up with her.

“I was wandering if we might talk?” he said in a rather quiet voice.

“Of course,” answered Melody, than told Eli to go ahead without her. “Well John, what is it you were wanting to talk about?" she asked. What on earth did he wish to speak with her about. Had he known about her and Ada eavesdropping?

"I have a favor to ask you," said John. He told her of his inheritance of his uncle's farm. She acted surprised, so she wouldn't give away her and Ada's secret.

"I would have asked Ada, but you know she's been to busy with her new beau," John replied.

Yes, she did know, Melody thought. Ada did spend most of her free time with Ray. Yesterday after church was the first in what seemed like forever that her and Ada had time to talk. She supposed Ada would marry Ray when she finished school this spring. Then Melody would be even more lonely. After all Ada wouldn't want to look for kittens, or any of the other fun stuff the two did together. No, she'll want to start a family, and be all caught up in her housework.

“Melody,” John said to get her attention from her daydreaming. “Like I said, I’m getting my uncle’s farm.”

“Yes, replied Melody, but why does that concern me?”

“Well, he said, I was wandering if you might help me?” he asked.

“Help you how?” surely he didn’t want her to gather eggs for him, did he? She thought.

“The house needs a female touch. You know curtains and such,” he said as his face turned red. “My uncle never being married, didn’t worry about such things.”

“Well what do you want me to do about it?” asked Melody.

“If I bring you the measurements, would you help me to pick out the material and make curtains and things?” he asked shyly.

"Oh sure, I guess I could help you. When would you like to get started?" she quickly asked.

"Next week, if possible. I'm going to Peoria this weekend, to help my uncle move some things. I'll be able to take the measurements and make the list of items I think we will need," John said excitedly.

"Very well, if you are sure you want me to," Melody replied. She didn't have anything else to spend her days doing. Since this was the last year of school for her, she didn't have much studying to do. She thought she might as well make curtains. It would be more interesting than anything else she could find to do.

As they parted John yelled back to her, "I'll pay you for your time and thanks."

"Sure," she yelled back. On the way home she wandered, what a strange request was that of John's.

When she got home, she found she still had some time before the six o'clock evening meal. She sat down by where Murphy was lying, and begin telling him of her day.

"Murphy, I don't know what to think. There are other girls around who sew far better than I. Most of them would love to sew for someone as handsome as John. Many girls in her school had a crush on him. Why would he ask me? And why does he care if his house has pretty things? His uncle wasn't married and he didn't care. I wander what the house is like? Maybe John will ask me go along with him sometime. I'd really like to see Illinois."

Melody didn't realize that her two brothers were hiding behind a big old lilac bush listening to her talk to Murphy.

The next day at school Eli found John studying by the tree. When he made sure Melody was no where to be found, he had a talk with John. "John, I know something you might be interested in knowing," laughed Eli.

"What could you know that I don't, Eli?" questioned John.

"I know that my sister wants to go with you to Peoria!" laughed Eli as he ran away.

John sat there with a puzzled look on his face. Melody wants to go to Peoria with me? That must mean she feels the same for me as I do for her. For the first time John admitted to himself that he really had feelings for her. He wandered to himself about her. He had always thought, she thought he was dull. And she would hardly look at him in the face after he winked at her. He was hoping that if they spent time together shopping for the house, she would decide he wasn't so bad.

At church that Sunday John found Melody.

"Melody, I have the measurements. Would you like to have dinner at our house? Then we can talk about our plans?' John quietly asked. "Sure, I'll ask my mother and father," she replied.

Her parents agreed to her request. As she was on her way home with John, a strange thought entered her. She had been a guest at the McFarland's farm many times, but this time she was not Ada's guest. She was John's. In fact Ada would not even be there. She was having dinner with Ray's family today. She had an odd feeling in her stomach. It was kind of like the feeling she had in the sixth grade, when she had to give the opening speech before the Christmas program.

"Would you like to take a walk?" asked John.

"Sure, I need to stretch after such a fine meal," she said as she smiled at Mrs. McFarland. John's mother was a great cook. Melody always enjoyed tasting her fine cooking. She daydreamed again. How will John ever find a wife that cooks as well as his mother? Poor guy, I guess he had better love her a lot to leave his mother's cooking.

"Melody, John asked, are you ready to go now?"

"Oh, yes, I was just thinking," she said. I have really got to stop this daydreaming she thought to herself.

As they walked, John began singing, "Back home in Indiana, and it seems that I can see, the gleaming candle light still shining bright thru the sycamores for me." Truly John had a beautiful voice, Melody thought. He always got the lead singing parts in the school programs. “Soon you’ll have to sing an Illinois song,” she reminded him.

“Yes, but I’ll always love coming back home to Indiana. Although Illinois isn’t much different. But, I will miss those I care about,” he said as he stopped and looked down at her.

Why was he looking at her so weird, she thought? Does he have something caught in his throat?

“John,” she said to shake the daze from him, “let’s talk about what material patterns you would be interested in.”

“I don’t really know, what do you like?” he asked.

“Well it doesn’t really matter what I like, it’s your house,” she answered. “I don’t know what women like in a house,” John answered nervously.

“What do you mean?” she puzzled. Surely he wasn’t getting married soon, she thought.

“Well, if I were to get married, I mean. I would want things to look nice for her,” he said timidly.

“ How nice, but I would think she would like to pick out her own things,” she said. “But, if you insist. I think a yellow checked pattern for the kitchen window. It’s so cheerful. There is nothing I dislike worse than a dark kitchen. And for the living room, not knowing what type of furniture you have, I was thinking of a delicate floral pattern with tie backs and floor length sheers. Something to let lots of light in.” She went on and on about colors and patterns.

“I knew you would have some great ideas, that is why I picked you,” John said.

They talked for several hours about different choices. John described all the furniture that was left in the house. That was only a few chairs and a sideboard with a hutch. He suggested they might go shopping for some added pieces.

When it was time to leave for Melody's he opened the door for her in his 1932 Ford. He was proud of his car. Even though it had been handed down from his father. His father had bought it new in 1932 and paid five hundred and twenty dollars for it. But, John kept it very well, you couldn't tell that it was used by a farmer.

As they got to Melody's house, John was telling her how much be enjoyed their evening together.

"Will you come for dinner again next Sunday?" he asked.

"It's your turn to be invited to mine, how about it, Sunday dinner?" she asked.

"Great," John answered smiling, "but can I pick you up on Saturday afternoon also. I was thinking we could go into town and look for some pieces for our house."

"I'd love to," she answered cheerfully. It sounded like a lot of fun. Going into town was one thing that Melody looked forward to. Even though there were very few shops and only one small diner.

Melody decided to sit and talk to Murphy for a while before going in. "Murphy, I just had the most wonderful afternoon."

In fact lately all the days have been wonderful, she thought. She hadn't been staying late in bed, dreading the day. In all honesty she couldn't wait for each new day to begin. Why, she marveled. What had changed? She thought for a while. Was it because each day she was thinking of John?

"No, It couldn't be," she said to Murphy. "John and I are just friends, that's all."

Then why did he get all red when talks to her? And why did she get nervous eating dinner at his house? And why does he refer to the Peoria house as our house? She thought.

"I wonder what it would be like to marry John and go to Peoria? Even if it's just a farm. It would be our farm. I could decorate it however I wish. But, I'm doing that already. John had said that he wanted it decorated in case he got married. You don't suppose, do you Murphy?"

Saturday arrived and John came to pick her up around one o'clock. They went to the only furniture store in town. There were many beautiful pieces of furniture. The man at the store greeted them smiling. “Hello, how may I help you today?” he asked.

“We’re looking for some furniture. Probably the most important would be a table and chairs set,” John said shyly.

“Oh yes, a must for every newly wed. And how long have you two been married?” the salesman asked.

Melody’s eyes got as big as plums. John’s face turned red.

“We’re not married sir. Just shopping together, that’s all,” said John as he smiled.

“That’s fine. No since waiting till after the wedding. So, when is the big day?” the salesman asked.

Melody jumped right in and replied, “We haven’t got a big day. We’re just shopping for HIS house.”

"Whatever you say dear," chuckled the salesman.

Melody was in deep thought all day. She couldn't believe he thought they were married. How embarrassing. And John, he actually thought it was funny. He laughed all the way home. Well, it was a little funny, she finally admitted to herself. Imagine her and John McFarland married.

Sunday after church, John joined Melody's family for dinner. She wandered if he had butterflies in his stomach, the way she had at his house. She was still quite embarrassed over the store owner mistaking them for a married couple. She came to the conclusion that they never did convince him they were only friends. Or were they only friends, she pondered. John didn't seem a bit nervous. He was very well mannered and her parents seemed to adore him. Even Eli and Ben acted as if they enjoyed his company.

∪

Melody arrived at school early Monday morning. It was the day before graduation. All the seniors were excited. John and Ada were graduating also. Even though they were siblings. John was nineteen and Ada eighteen. John was held back a year because he had scarlet fever in the fourth grade. Although Melody didn't remember much about it. After all, who can remember things that happened in the third grade. Ada was to give the speech since she would be graduating with the highest grades. They all knew it would be Ada with the highest grades. She always held the top scores for as long as any could recall. There were only eleven seniors to graduate Tuesday night.

Five of the boys that would be seniors enlisted in the army. Everyone was in a happy mood, although rumors of the draft filled the air.

The seniors had been presented each with a school day autograph book. All day they were being exchanged among them. Melody couldn't wait to get home and read her's over with Murphy.

"Murphy, I received my senior memory book, want to hear the writings?" she asked, even though he ad no choice in the matter. Murphy often had to hear her stories and thoughts whether he wanted to or not.

Dear Melody, True friends are like diamonds, precious and rare, false friends are awful, found everywhere, you're a diamond, your friend Virginia.

Dear Melody, In your golden chain of friendship, please regard me as a link, Lemore

Dear Melody, When in some far and distant land you view this writing of my hand, although my face you cannot see, My dearest friend remember me! Ada

Dear Melody, As sure as the vine grows around the stump, you will always be my sugar lump, Love John

"His sugar lump, what in the world does he mean by that Murphy? You don't think, that he thinks of me as his girl, do you? She questioned Murphy. Melody read it again.

"As sure as the vine grows around the stump you will always be my sugar lump, love John. What is a sugar lump. And he wrote love. Look

Murphy right there. It says love John," Melody said and continued to read more.

Melody, when you get married and live up stairs for goodness sakes don't eat cat hairs. Maxine

Dear Melody, when you get married and have girl twins, don't call on me for didy pins, Wayne.

"Who on earth do they think I'm going to marry? You don't suppose it's John do you? I can't imagine where they'd get an idea like that? We do spend a lot of time together, but it's not like that. Is it Murphy?"

Dear Melody, When the golden sun is sinking and your path no longer trod, may you name in gold be written, in the autograph of God. Norma

Dear Melody, may God bless you and keep you from all sin, and when you knock at the Golden gate, may the angels say "Come in", Manda

Dear Melody, when you get marred may your paths be filled with roses and all your kids have turned up noses, Lucille.

"Another comment of getting married. Well Murphy, these sayings shall be our secrets. I would hate to think what would happen if my brothers got wind of this," she whispered to Murphy.

Tuesday evening was graduation. It was at eight o'clock. Melody had sent a few invitations, but didn't expect any to show up. People didn't have a lot of extra money for gas, with the war going on. Most of her family lived in Indiana, but still quite a driving distance. After the ceremony, John asked to drive her home. Her house was a short way from the school, so gas was not a problem. They talked about the house on the ride home. Melody was beginning to feel like it was almost hers. John told her that his uncle had been checking on it while he was in school. Now that he had graduated, he wanted to start living there as soon as he had all the things he needed.

"There are a few things I need to get before moving. We still have to find some furniture," he said. On there journey to town, they found most things were too expensive. He had to save most of his money for the livestock. He told her he was going to work a month or so, at Edward Harris' livestock farm. This would give him ten dollars a week for extras. Edward was Ada's beau Ray's father.

Summer was filled with making things for the house. She had completed the kitchen curtains. She even had enough material left for a matching table cloth. Since no table had been purchased yet, she guessed on the size. Her mother was teaching her to embroidery on pieces for napkins. Melody was quite proud of her handy work. John asked to see them, but she wanted him to wait till the kitchen set was completed. She couldn't wait to surprise him with all that she had done.

John continued to work for the Harris' for the summer. Melody missed not seeing him every day as she did when they were in school. On occasion they would go into town where dances were held. The big dance of the time was the swing. They had a great time. Ada and Ray would often join them and help with the gas expense. Melody had to admit she loved it when John held her close on the dance floor. It was the most exciting time she could ever remember having. She felt unlike she had ever felt before.

September came and Melody was working hard trying to keep up with her mother. They were in late harvest time. That meant canning and more canning. Melody dreaded shucking the corn. But, at least she could do that outside and talk to Murphy the same time. She sometimes wished she had more schooling left. She pondered on how her mother ever managed to keep the chores up when she was away at school. Melody looked forward to sundays more than ever. This was the only day that she could rest from the storing of food. And mostly she would get to see John. How odd she thought, it used to be she looked forward to seeing Ada and now it was John.

Though the treat of war was deep in everyone's heart, the farm still went on as usual. She prayed daily that the fighting would end soon. At night after the evening meal her family would listen to the radio for the latest news. Things didn't sound good at all.

John worked for the Harris' throughout the fall also. They greatly needed his help on the farm. The two regular boys, who worked there, joined the army. So John felt only right about staying until they could find other help.

Thanksgiving dinner was held at Melody's. Her family from Bloomington joined them. John also came by later after a meal with his family. She was so proud as she introduced him to her family. Everyone was impressed with his wonderful personalty. Most all that day was filled with talks of the war. Melody wished they would talk of something else. But, since it was affecting all their lives. It seemed to be the subject chosen. She did manage to catch a few minutes of talk with John about the house.

On December 7, 1941 as the family listened to radio, they heard the terrible news. Japan had bombed Pearl Harbor, a Hawaiian island. A total of 2,323 were killed. America was now full in war. The news frightened Melody deep within her. A fear like none she had ever had. Thank God, she thought, that Ben and Eli were too young, to realize what it meant. She wondered how the families of those who lost their lives felt. Did they even know yet who were dead? Did the families just have to wait and wonder? Melody cried that night as she had never done before. How horrible not to even expect anything and then as fast as a snap of the finger, that community was hit. Did any of them have time to run? Were there any children there? Was her family safe in Indiana? Could they get bombed? There were so many questions she felt.

The rooster crowed loudly as Melody was searching for her purse Sunday morning. She looked out the window.

"I beat you this time old rooster. I was up long before you!" she laughed.

A few days had passed since the Pearl Harbor night. She wasn't feeling as gloom and scared. In fact she was excited about going to church today. She couldn't wait to tell John about a second hand store where they could get the needed furniture.

As they pulled up at church, Melody noticed a crowd of people gathered around the McFarlands. What in the world is going on, she thought. When she got out of the car, Ada ran to her.

"Ada, what's wrong?" Melody asked frightened.

"It's John, oh Melody, he wanted to drive to your house, but the letter was late, and . . . ? Ada was trying to talk but crying too hard.

"Ada what is you trying to say? Has John been hurt? Tell me Ada, tell me!" Melody said as she shook both of Ada's arms.

"John's been drafted!" cried Ada.

Melody's heart sank. She knew it was possible. John was nineteen, healthy and unmarried. She didn't want to believe it was true. What about Peoria? What about her? It was so unfair. The war she hated so much had now taken John away from her. What had started to be a glorious day turned out to be the worst day of her life.

The days dragged by again. All she could think about was John. She feared he would get killed. A few boys in her neighborhood had already died. What if something like Pearl Harbor happens again? The only one whom she felt she could turn to was Murphy.

"Oh Murphy, you don't know how blessed you are. Dogs don't have wars. All you have to worry about is.....well nothing. All your needs are filled. Murphy what will happen if John doesn't come back? I just don't know if I could ever be happy again if that were to happen. Murphy, I miss him so much," Melody sobbed.

A few days later, a letter arrived.

"Melody, you have a letter! It's marked Junction City Kansas!" her mother exclaimed. Her mother hoped it would be good news. She hated to see her daughter in such woe.

"It's got to be from John!" Melody said as she smiled and took the letter to the hayloft to read.

Once in the loft she read the envelope, Junction City Kansas, Dec. 1941.

Dear Melody, I am writing this on the bus. I am so sorry for not telling you goodbye. Things

happened so fast. This is a busy place. I am going to at Fort Riley, camp Forsyth for training. It is nothing like the farm in Indiana. Please don't forget about me. I will write again when I know what is going on. Love John.

Melody spent the rest of the day crying and thinking in the hayloft. This couldn't be happening. She had been so happy. Now she felt as if her heart had been ripped from her chest. Why did he have to leave? It wasn't fair. John had so many dreams and plans. And so had she.

When she arrived at church the next Sunday, she noticed Ada was waiting outside. She was all smiles. Melody couldn't help but hope it meant John was coming home. Maybe it was all a big mistake, she thought. Maybe John was coming home and everything would be as it once was.

"Melody come here! I've got some exciting news!" exclaimed Ada. "What?" asked Melody excitedly.

"Look," Ada said as she held out her hand. "Ray asked me to marry him. He was going to wait till Christmas day, but just couldn't. He thought it would cheer me up after John left. Boy, was he right, I'm happier than I've ever been."

"Oh, it's just lovely," Melody said as she was trying to hold back the tears.

"But, of course I told him we would have to wait till John comes home," Ada said not realizing how sadden Melody was.

She could hardly wait to get home and pour her feelings out to Murphy.

"Well Murphy, Ada is getting married. I really am an old maid. I bet that Ray just wants to get married, thinking he'll avoid the draft." Of course she knew that wasn't true. She had known for a long time how Ray felt about Ada. In fact she was surprised that he hadn't asked her sooner.

"Maybe I should get a job. That will keep me busy. But how? I'm way here with no car. Maybe this week when we go to Christmas dinner at Aunt Rose's I'll ask if she might know of some employment in Bloomington and I could stay with her," she told the dog.

The rest of the day her thoughts were of a job. What would it be like to move away from home? How often would she get to see her family? Would it be much different from living on the farm? Would she miss Murphy too much?

Monday afternoon the mail car drove up. The mail man saw Melody in the yard and motioned for her to come over.

He yelled to her, "Hey girlie, I think I got another letter for you. I believe it's from your beau at Fort Riley."

Melody had always thought the mail carrier was far too nosy and she didn't like it when he referred to her as girlie. Didn't he realize she was all grown up.

Sure enough the letter was from John. It read,

Dear Melody, It looks as though I'll miss Christmas with you. I don't have much to say. Could you please write to me? Take care. Don't forget about me. Love John.

It was true. She hadn't even thought about writing him. She was so lost in her own sorrow that she forgot about his.

"I'll take care of this right now," she told Murphy who was at her side as always. Then she left for her room. She sat on her bed wondering what to write. She didn't want to seem sad or it might bring him more sorrow. Though she didn't want to seem happy or he might think she didn't miss him. I'll just write about the house in Peoria. That will give him something to look forward to. So she wrote;

Dear John, I miss you very much. I am looking forward to your return so we can finish our plans on the house. Everyone says Hi, and we miss you dearly. Please don't forget us Hoosiers. Love Melody.

She prayed every night that he would return home soon.

Christmas day came with a strong chill. The family went to Aunt Rose's in Bloomington. All her cousins, aunts and uncles were there. It didn't seem like Christmas to Melody. Usually she enjoyed it, but today all the talk was of war. She couldn't count how many times she was asked, where's that handsome young man that came to Thanksgiving? You need to hang onto that one, some said. But, how could she hang on, when war took him she asked herself. She was sick with war. Why does this have to happen, she wondered? Even if she didn't have a good time, she wasn't going to ruin Christmas for Murphy. She planned on taking him home some food scraps. His Christmas would be special, even if hers wasn't.

Early in the evening Melody's father announced they needed to be leaving. Snow was beginning to fall and he wanted to get home before it got dangerous.

"Aunt Rose, can I take the turkey bones home for Murphy, please?" she asked.

"I swear girl, you take better care of that dog than you do yourself," commented Aunt Rose. "But of course you can, and don't forget this week's paper you wanted. If you are looking for a job and get one, your more than welcome to stay here. Just don't bring Murphy," Aunt Rose said laughingly.

All the way home Melody couldn't wait to give Murphy her gift. The dog always got something special from Melody on the holidays. She thought she would sit with him while he enjoyed his feast and she would scan the paper for possible employment.

She sat down with Murphy in the barn.

"Murphy, I'm going to miss you dearly if I get a job. Aunt Rose says I take better care of you than myself. I suppose she is right. Just look at me. I don't fix myself up very much. I mean who will care on this farm what I look like. Maybe if I get a job, I'll purchase some new items to spruce myself up. I just wish you could go with me."

Weeks past and she had still not heard from John. The farm was truly dull this winter. The harvest was all finished. Mother didn't need her as much now that all the food had been stored. Fathers was no longer in the fields. He spent most of his time with Ben and Eli. They both got blue tick pups for Christmas. A female and male, they intended on making coon dogs out of. Almost every evening the three and the two dogs were out in the woods. Melody couldn't imagine her and Murphy trying to join them on such an adventure. Running though the woods like a crazy person.

One day Melody was deep in conversation with Murphy, when she heard the sound of a car. It was too early for the mail.

"Who could that be?" she asked Murphy as if he knew.

They didn't often get company, except on holidays and sundays. Just then she saw John's 32 Ford coming down the lane.

"Oh my Murphy, could it be?" As the car pulled up, she realized it wasn't John. It was Ada, her father, and Ray. Dear Lord please don't let it be something has happened to John, she prayed. Ada ran to her as bubbly as ever.

"Melody, I've missed you so much," said Ada. "You look as white as a ghost, is something wrong?"

"I just thought you were John, and when I realized it was you, I thought John was....dead," she cried.

"I'm sorry. I didn't think. Pa said we should drive it now and then, because if it sits too long it won't be of any good when John comes home," Ada said softly.

"It's all right. I'm glad to see you. What brings you by?" asked Melody. "Ray has bought the old Evans place, next to his father's. He and Pa are seeing if your father has any hogs he wants to sell. Ray says he wants to focus on having a hog farm. I told him it was fine with me as long as I don't have to mess with those nasty animals," Ada rattled on and on. She talked of all her decorating ideas. What kind of furniture was left in the place, stuff she had in her hope chest, and things she would need to get. Melody thought about how much she was like Ada not long ago, when John was home. After Ada's long talk of the house, she finally came around to talk of John.

"Have you heard from John?" asked Ada.

"No, not for weeks. I'm just worried he's been sent out," replied Melody.

"We haven't heard from him either. I wish there was a way to find out what's going on with him. We'll just have to pray that the Lord keeps him safe," assured Ada. "I'm sure the war can't last much longer." Before Ada left, she told

Melody that she and Ray planned a June wedding, depending on, of course, that John was back.

"Just think Murphy, in June Ada will be Mrs. Ray Harris. Oh, I am an old maid. I can't take it any longer. I have to get on with my life. I'm going to ask father and mother if I can go to Aunt Rose's and get a job.

She asked her mother and father at the evening meal. The evening meal was when the family would discuss events and questions. She assumed that is why her mother always made sure they all ate at the same time. They agreed she could try for a job, but asked that she waited till early spring. Melody thought that it sounded reasonable. She knew there would be plenty of jobs available with so many boys of to war. But, she also knew that meant little pay. Minimum wage was at forty-three cents an hour.

The next week a letter arrived for Melody, it read.

Dear Melody. I'm sorry I haven't wrote, but since the war is in full swing, my time is slim. They have been pushing us hard on our training. How are you? I don't like it here. It is so cold and raining. I would like to be home, but I hear soon I will be shipped out. I don't know where, but I have heard it will probably be Sicily, Europe or Pacific. I will understand if you find a beau. After all I never actually asked you to be mine. Until I get home, I will just sing, Back home in Indiana. Love John.

Melody's heart felt dead after reading the letter. He sounded so sad. What did the letter mean? Was he saying he never had any intention of ever being her beau? Or did he mean that he just assumed he was? Melody felt more confused and miserable than ever.

◡

Melody left for Bloomington early in the spring of 1942. She cried as she kissed Murphy on the head. She assured him she would be home as much as possible and would try to find a way to take him next time.

Aunt Rose was very happy to have her stay. She had found her a job at a sewing factory. It wasn't really the kind of work that Melody liked. But, sewing was much needed for war time supplies. Weeks passed and she had made a few friends, but none that she like better than Murphy. Aunt Rose was always nagging at her to go to some of the dances. It just didn't seem right of Melody, thinking of John off fighting a war and her dancing.

One of her co workers was a guy named Seth Perry. He was always making it a point to talk to her. She assumed he was in management, because of the way he dressed. He always wore the latest fashions. That usually meant a double-breasted jacket and cream colored shirt. On occasion he would add a Stetson looking hat. Melody disliked the days that he bothered her. He reminded her of the flies that hung around when they made molasses on the farm. There was nothing she could do to drive him away.

She did enjoy the church her and Aunt Rose visited. It was much bigger than the one at home. The minister was louder to. His voice made your hair stand up on end. She enjoyed all the sights of Sunday. The nice way people dressed and wore their hair. They did dress a lot more stylish than the people back home. She listened very little to the sermons. She was to busy looking at all the people. But, on one Sunday she heard something that interest her. It was something her mother always had said. The preacher had said rejoice in this day that the Lord has made. Melody sat straight up and listened.

He said, "This is the day that the Lord has made, rejoice and be glad. God decided you were to live today. You woke up this morning and were alive! He made this day, not for you to sit and sorrow. But, for you to rejoice and be glad. You are alive today to be a servant of God, and no other reason. Do not take pity on yourself, be glad. If you take this day or any other day and sulk in you own sorrow than you have not done any good for you or the Lord. A happy heart makes the face cheerful. A cheerful heart is good medicine, read it in Proverbs! What this country needs are more happy hearts and cheerful faces.

Melody listened, like she had never listened before. He was right. Why hadn't she seen it before? She had gone to church all her life, and yet she never realized this. And all this time her mother had been telling her the same thing. But, she was just too stubborn to listen. She felt a feeling of peace and beauty.

On the walk home, she realized all the beauty she had been missing. She had God in her heart and a new life with Christ. All the sorrows and self pity she had been feeling were gone.

Next week came and Melody went to work as usual. She had been feeling good about the new aspect she had on life. Although Seth Perry had been hanging around her more than his usual, she felt as if she could handle it. She just kept trying to remind herself of something she had read in the Bible, bear with each other. And then the one about love thy neighbor. It was really hard for her, but she did try. He really thought he was something great, Melody thought. She couldn't figure why he hadn't been drafted. She guess his number hadn't come up. He was a little older, possibly in his mid twenties. Maybe they took the younger ones first, she decided.

On Friday when Seth found Melody he asked, " I was wandering if you would like to go dancing tonight with me?"

"Well, I really don't feel much like dancing, but thank you anyway," she tried to say politely.

"We could go out for dinner, I'll pick you up at seven," he said in a pushy sort of way.

"No, I really don't think I can. I need to spend some time with my aunt," Melody softly said.

"Don't tell me you've got yourself one of those war heroes?" he rudely asked.

Melody felt angry. How dare he act that way about the military boys. "As a matter of fact, Mr. Perry, I do. And I am very proud of him fighting for his country," she replied, this time not so softly.

"You really think he'll come back for you, don't you? Well girl, you don't know what you're missing not going out with me. Your hero is never coming back. He'll either get himself killed, or find him another pretty girlie," he laughed.

Melody was never so mad. She stood up and slapped him right in his face. He looked shocked, but than informed her that she was now FIRED! That was all right with her, she thought. She would never work for somebody as rude as that. As she left, she got the last laugh. She told him a bit of news he might be interested in. They had just raised the draft age to 35. She was told later by her Aunt that Seth quit his job and just disappeared. The rumor was that he headed up north, way up north.

Melody had to start her job search again. But, she didn't have to look long. Late one afternoon they received a call on the telephone. It was from a neighbor of her parents. It seemed her mother had taken a bad fall and broken her leg. Melody's family was wondering if she would like to come home and help out. Of course she went home as soon as possible. She couldn't wait to see Murphy and tell him of her adventures. She also had actually missed the farm. Isn't it funny that all this time I tried to leave and when I do I miss it, she thought to herself.

She had plenty to keep her busy. Her mother's leg was a very bad break. She needed to be completely off it for at least two months and then she would only be able to be on it for short periods of time. Melody knew that if she hadn't made it home, that her mother would have tried to get up.

It was hard work for Melody. She was always washing clothes in the wash tub it seemed. The mending of the clothes was every day also. It appeared Eli and Ben were forever ripping their clothes on those wild coon hunts. The blue tick hounds had a litter of pups. Eight of them running everywhere. Melody had to watch the wash basket very close. Those little pups would sneak up and steal clothes right out of it. They would drag them all around the yard. Then she would have to wash them all over again. She asked her brothers to keep them put up, but the pups always managed to sneak out. Things were really hard for her. In May they had to start gas rations, which meant only three gallons a week for regular vehicles. And in August most of the country was going through meatless days. It didn't affect the farm as much as it did people in the cities. Melody was glad she was back home in the safety of the farm.

Melody's parents were so happy to hear about how the sermon had changed her feelings of life. They had noticed the change in her. She told them of Seth Perry and the situation that lead to her firing. Although they did not approve of her slapping, they couldn't say they wouldn't have done the same thing in her case.

She received a letter from Ada along with an invitation. She had decided to get married. They had already postponed the wedding since their June plans. Ada explained they would like to wait on John, but the war could last for years. They needed to get on with their lives. The wedding was to be a Christmas wedding set for December 23.

Melody was glad for Ada. She had waited a long time for John to return. It was already 1942 and in about a month it would be 1943. Time was flying by. No one had heard from John. There had been rumors that he was missing in action. Or maybe he was a prisoner of war. Melody feared he was dead.

December 23, 1942. It was a beautiful day. Ada looked radiant. But, still Melody noticed a hint of sadness in Ada's eyes. Of course it was the longing for her brother. Ada's mother and father cried that day also. Melody wondered how many of those tears were really being cried for John. The happy couple didn't go on a honeymoon vacation. They didn't feel they could afford the trip. And there would not be enough gas stamps to have gone far anyway. Instead they went back to the farm Ray had purchased nearly a year ago for him and Ada.

◡

Christmas was very busy for Melody, since her mother was to stay off her leg. The family decided to gather at their farm rather than Aunt Rose's house.

Aunts, uncles and cousins filled the Jones' modest farm house. Food was plentiful even with the rationing going on. Melody figured her aunts must have saved up for the big day. Even though the talk was still of war, she enjoyed this Christmas. It was the best she could ever remember. This Christmas she was rejoicing the birth of Christ and it felt great, even if everyone was talking about the war. Melody had a wonderful feeling in her heart that nothing could destroy. She was so happy to have the chance of visiting Aunt Rose. They still got a big laugh when they talked of Seth Perry.

After the company was left, and the clean up was done, Melody went to spend time with Murphy. She had saved him a nice big turkey drumstick and a slice of ham. She had hid the drumstick as the guest were arriving in the pantry under some apples in a crate. No one noticed it missing.

"Oh Murphy, I do spoil you. But, than I have no one else to spoil. I wonder, do you know Christ? He knows you," she said.

Melody held Murphy for a long while that night, thinking of the joy she felt. Then she got up to leave.

"Good night, and merry Christmas," she whispered to him.

As Melody sat on her bed, she thought of John. She wondered where he was spending his Christmas. Did he even know it was Christmas? He may not. Or he may be with Christ. Oh, Lord I do love him so, please watch over him. She than said her prayers and went to sleep.

1943 was here. Had it been that long since John left? She thought to herself. The war was still going on. Her mother was getting better, but still needed her help. Melody decided to stay on the farm. She promised to let God decide where and when she was to leave.

The months went by and still no word from John. She tried to keep her days busy. Ada often invited her over to help with some chore of some sort. But, Melody felt it was just Ada's way of trying to keep herself and Melody's mind off the war. Ada had told her that deep within she feared that Ray could be drafted.

One unusually cold September day, Melody was on her way for her daily chat with Murphy. He was in the barn snuggling in the hay, trying to stay away from the blue ticks. As she was heading to the barn, the mail car pulled up.

"Something you've been waiting on young lady," said the carrier. He no longer referred to her as "Girlie." Now she was a young lady.

Something I've been waiting on? What could it be? she thought. When she got to the box, she found a letter from John.

Dear Melody, I've missed you so much. It is hard to get a letter out of here. Things are so messed up. I don't even know if this will reach you. You may have found somebody else or even be married. I hope you are well. Don't bother writing, we move so much, it will never reach me. Love John.

His letter was short. There was no return address. At least she knew he was alive. She would have liked to wrote him back and tell him how she had found God in her life. She also wanted to tell him that she loved him. The love for him was something she never would have believed two years ago. She realized now that he was gone, how much she cared for him. She couldn't wait for his return to let him know. But, for now it would have to wait. Poor John, she thought, he doesn't even know how I feel or even that Ada had gotten married.

◡

Melody's days were as busy as ever. Since so many of the neighbor boys had left, her father was short handed. This meant that she and her brothers would have to help put up hay and various other farm duties. Not only that but all their other regular chores had to be done. Melody was glad no boys were around to see her wearing a pair of her father's old work pants. What a sight John McFarland would have seeing me in this outfit.

When October was near over, she felt as exhausted as she had ever had. Ben and Eli both needed more clothes made for school. They were growing so fast she couldn't sew fast enough. The family included the McFarland's at their Thanksgiving dinner this year. The talk was mostly of John. But, Ada did have some exiting news for Melody. She was expecting her and Ray's first child. She told Melody if the baby was a boy they planned to name him John. She was not surprised at all, she knew that Ada and Ray had wanted to start a family right away. She was truly surprised it took as long as it did. Genuinely she was happy for the couple.

That evening as her little tradition went, she went to see Murphy. She had his surprise dinner for him.

"Murphy, Ada is going to be a mother. I'm so happy for her. You know Ada has always had it all. She has nice looks, smarts, and now a husband and a baby on the way. I guess I do feel a little jealous. But, I suppose it has not been God's will for me to have such things. I know I have always said I didn't want to live on a farm. But, you know, I can't imagine life doing anything else. After all, I did move to Bloomington and still while I was there, I longed to be here. Does that make sense Murphy? She asked the dog as he gobbled his meal down.

Christmas was very festive. The family went to Bloomington. Melody was so happy to see Aunt Rose.

"Melody, I was thinking, if you would like to come and live with me again? I would be more than happy to have you here," Aunt Rose asked. "We'll I've decided to let God choose when and if I should leave the farm," she replied.

"How will you know that ?" responded Rose.

"I will feel it in my heart and then I will know that it is what God wishes for me to do," Melody said with an upbeat of joy.

When the family returned home, she went out to see Murphy and present him with his holiday treat.

"Murphy, I hope your Christmas was merry. Mine was. You know what? Even though, I don't have any plans, and I am sort of an old maid, I can't help but feel joy this Christmas. I know I am alive and well because God has something planned for me. I don't know what it is yet. But, isn't it exciting to think about what it might be. It's like one of those adventures that unroll a little each day. You know what I mean?" she smiled and kissed him goodnight. She went to sleep that night with peace and joy in her heart.

July 1944, John E. Harris was born. Ada's dad came over that very day to announce the good news. He was glowing with happiness. A week later Melody went to see the new arrival.

"Oh, Ada, he is just beautiful. I'm so happy for you," Melody delightfully said.

"Here you want to hold him, after all you might be his aunt someday," laughed Ada.

"I don't know, you see I really don't know how John feels about me. He might even find someone else. He never actually said how he felt, you know," she replied as she looked down at baby John in her arms. "Melody, wake up. I saw the way John always looked at you. And before he left, you two spent nearly every day possible together. Don't forget it was you that he asked to help him," Ada reminded her.

"But, he would have asked you if you would have had more time. I was just the next available," Melody said softly.

"That's not true, I had time. In fact I even offered to help. But, he told me the only person that he wanted to help him was YOU," she responded.

"I didn't know. So, he said that I was the only one he wanted to help him?" asked Melody.

"That's right. Think about it. He could have asked anyone. He didn't even have to have it done either. He knew ma would see to it that he had all the essentials. He wanted you to help so he could be with you. It wasn't about curtains or furniture. Men could care less about that sort of stuff. It's you that he wants for his house in Peoria, not new curtains," Ada informed her.

"I never realized this. I mean, I feel so dumb. How could I have not seen it? Oh, I guess sometimes I wondered. But, I never really thought John could like me," she said surprisingly.

Melody went home that night glad for the talk with Ada. Just leave it Ada to come right out and tell it like it was she thought.

As the year strolled on Melody continued to think of Ada's comment. She was more excited than ever for John to return, if he returned at all. On her visits to see baby John and Ada her first question was always if anyone had heard from John. And always the answer was no.

1945 came and still the war continued. She spent a lot of time helping her father with the scrap drive. They had several storage buildings on the farm to be cleaned out. They could take some of the junk into town and get a little money. Although Melody felt sort of strange about taking money for scraps that were for the war effort. But never the less she knew her parents could use the money.

She also made as many trips possible to Ada's. She loved to watch little John, who was going fast. So far Ray had not been drafted. Ada seemed a little relieved after the baby was born. She didn't think they would take a married man who had a child. But, Melody wasn't too sure. She hoped Ada was right. She didn't think Ada or her parents could handle both Ray and John gone.

The family still listened to the radio each night for news of the war. One night in August there was a news breaking announcement. U.S. planes drop an atomic bomb on Hiroshima. Melody's face grew pale as did her parents. All sorts of thought raced through her mind. What if John was there? Does this mean the war is near over? Did he help drop the bomb? She was scared. So scared for John. She prayed and prayed that night. She prayed John's life was spared, but most of all that he knew God like she did.

September 1945, as the family listened to the radio, they heard the news the world had been waiting for. Japan surrenders, the war is over! Melody had never felt the way she felt that night. Her whole family held each other and cried. They cried until there were no tears left in them. They all prayed and thanked the Lord. Melody went to her room with a concerned heart. She heard on the radio they estimated the casualties of the war were millions upon millions. How sad for the families. Millions of people gone, she thought. How many of them knew God?

Melody so wished she knew where John was. She realized it would be a long time before any of the guys overseas would get to come home. She didn't know if John would even get to come home. What if he were a prisoner of war? What happens then? As the months passed, she found herself constantly looking in the mailbox, in hopes of hearing from John.

1946, and so far there had been a few boys return home. Some families were told the sad news that there loved ones were not coming home. They had been killed. Melody's heart went out to these people. But, at least they knew now. Neither her family nor the McFarlands knew what became of John. Many came home with missing legs, some were out of their minds, either way she would always love him and just wanted to know the answer. Where was John?

The days were long. Eli and Ben were usually in the woods running dogs or helping her father.

Her mother was back to her old self. And then there was dear Murphy, she could always count on him for company. She sat on the ground with him beside her.

"Murphy, do you wish you were running with those silly blue ticks? I suppose not. I've never seen you run to much. I guess if you wanted to, you would," she was rattling on.

"Are you still talking to that old dog?" a voice came from behind her. She turned around to find John McFarland standing there. She could not believe her eyes. Is it really him? She thought. She couldn't move. She just stood there in a gaze.

"Well aren't you happy to see me?" John laughed. It was him. John was alive and home. He walked to her, put his arms around her and held her, as they both cried and cried.

"Oh, John, I can't believe your home," she laughed.

"This was my first stop. I was hoping you were here," he said. "Melody, I have to know, did you find somebody else?" John asked quickly. "Well yes, sort of. His name is Jesus!" she answered.

"Oh yes, I meet him when I was overseas. Nice Guy, think he'd mind if I married you?" John asked as he gave her a wink.

"I don't think he would mind at all. In fact I think he will give us his blessing," she answered as they both laughed.

"What do you say, we get married and move to that farm in Peoria? Are you willing to be a farmer's wife?" he asked

"Yes, I truly am." She knew in her heart this was what God had planned for her. "But, only if you promise we can visit Murphy often. I will miss him dearly," she replied.

"Better than that, lets take him with us!" John gladly indicated.

Later that month, John and Melody were married. Melody felt as if her life was settled and complete. Now she and Murphy were on the best adventure of their lives.

The End.

About the Author

Lori Ellett Street was born in Linton, Indiana. She is married and has two children. Lori devotes most of her time to writing and church activities.

www.ingramcontent.com/pod-product-compliance
Ingram Content Group UK Ltd.
Pitfield, Milton Keynes, MK11 3LW, UK
UKHW040017200726
13854UKWH00001B/246

9 780759 610125